D0852777

dick bruna

miffy's dream

SIMON AND SCHUSTER
London New York Sydney Toronto New Delhi

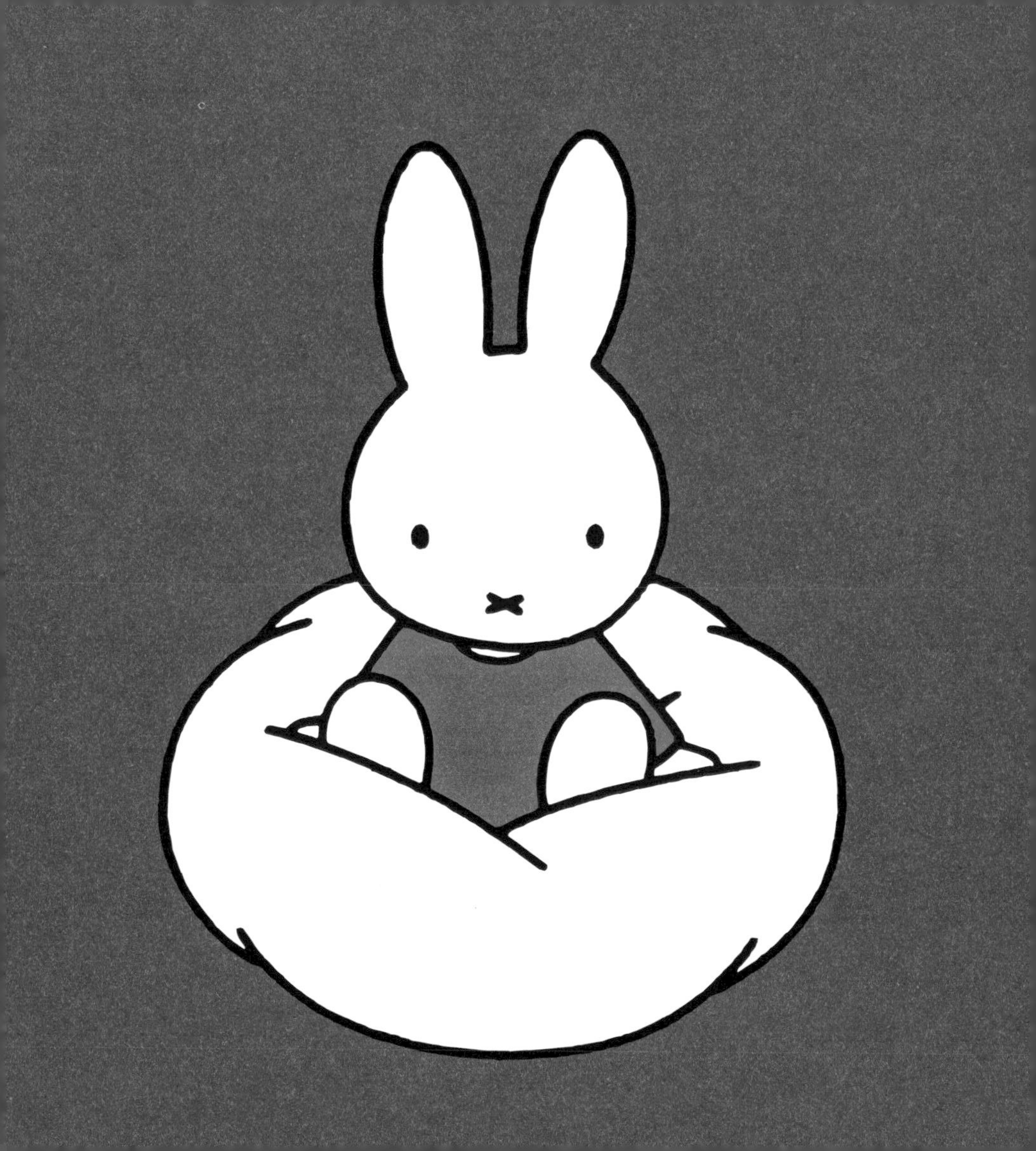

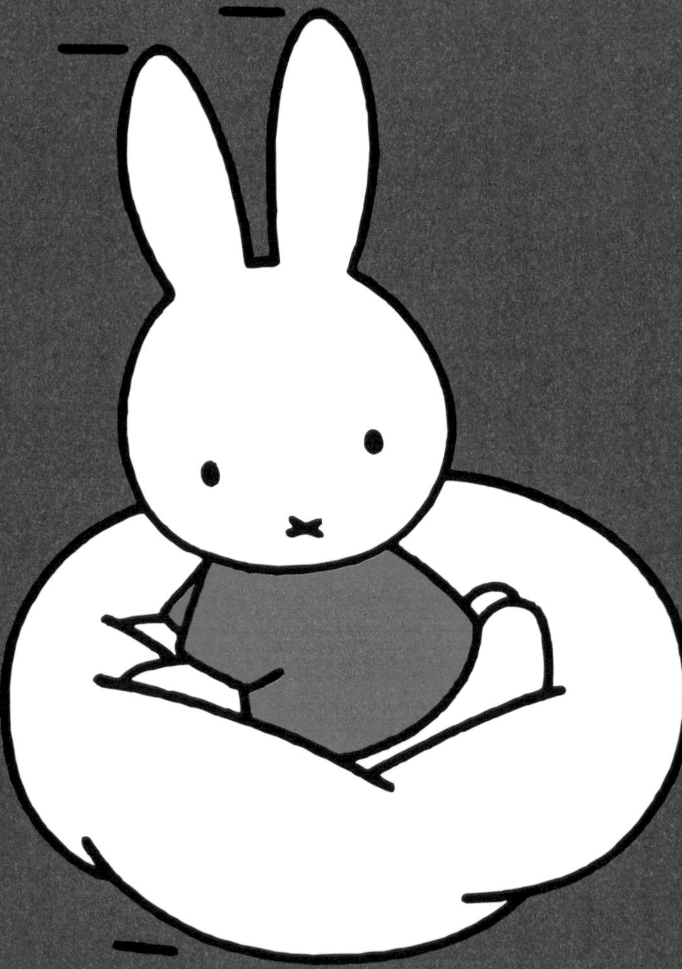

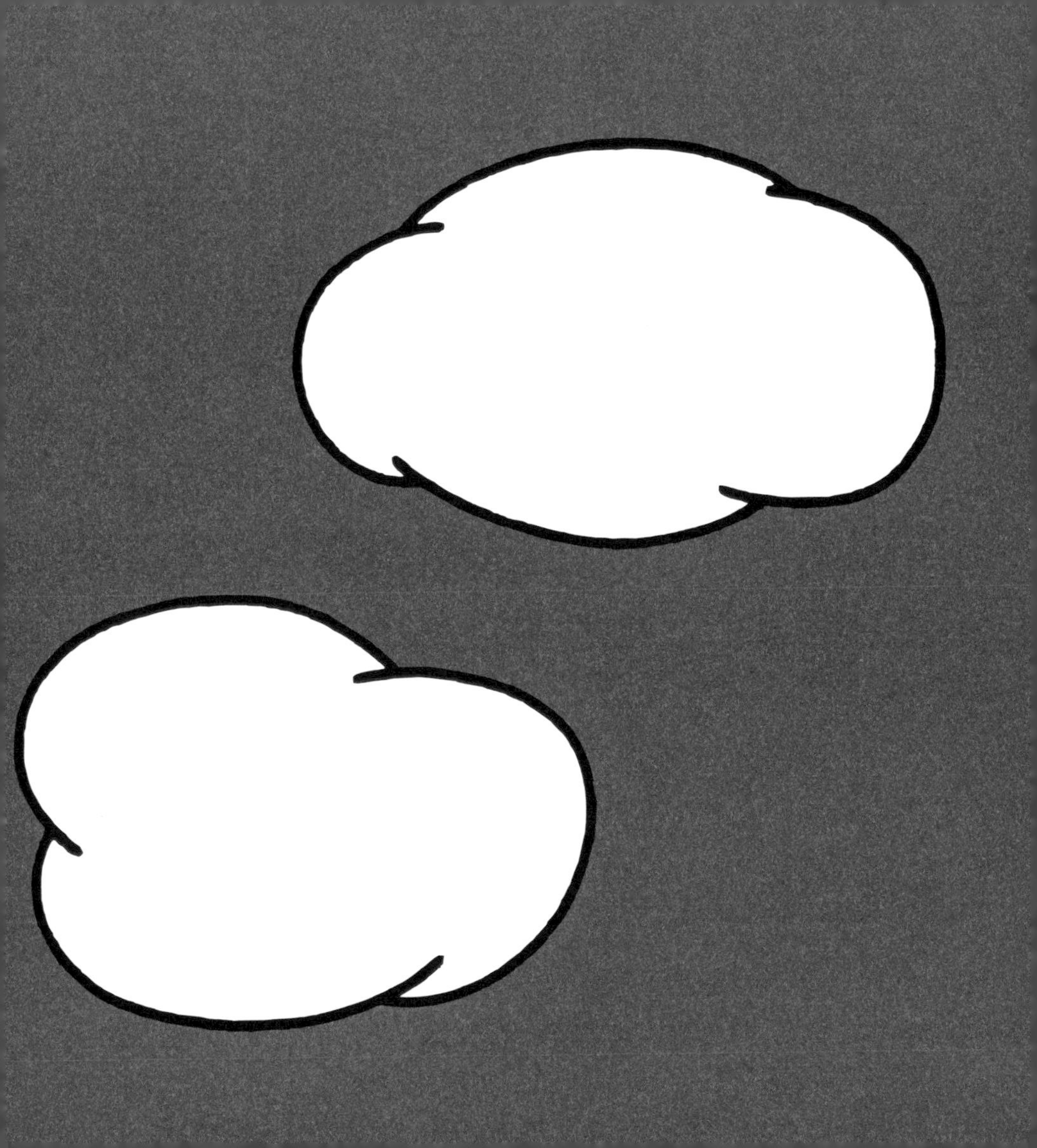

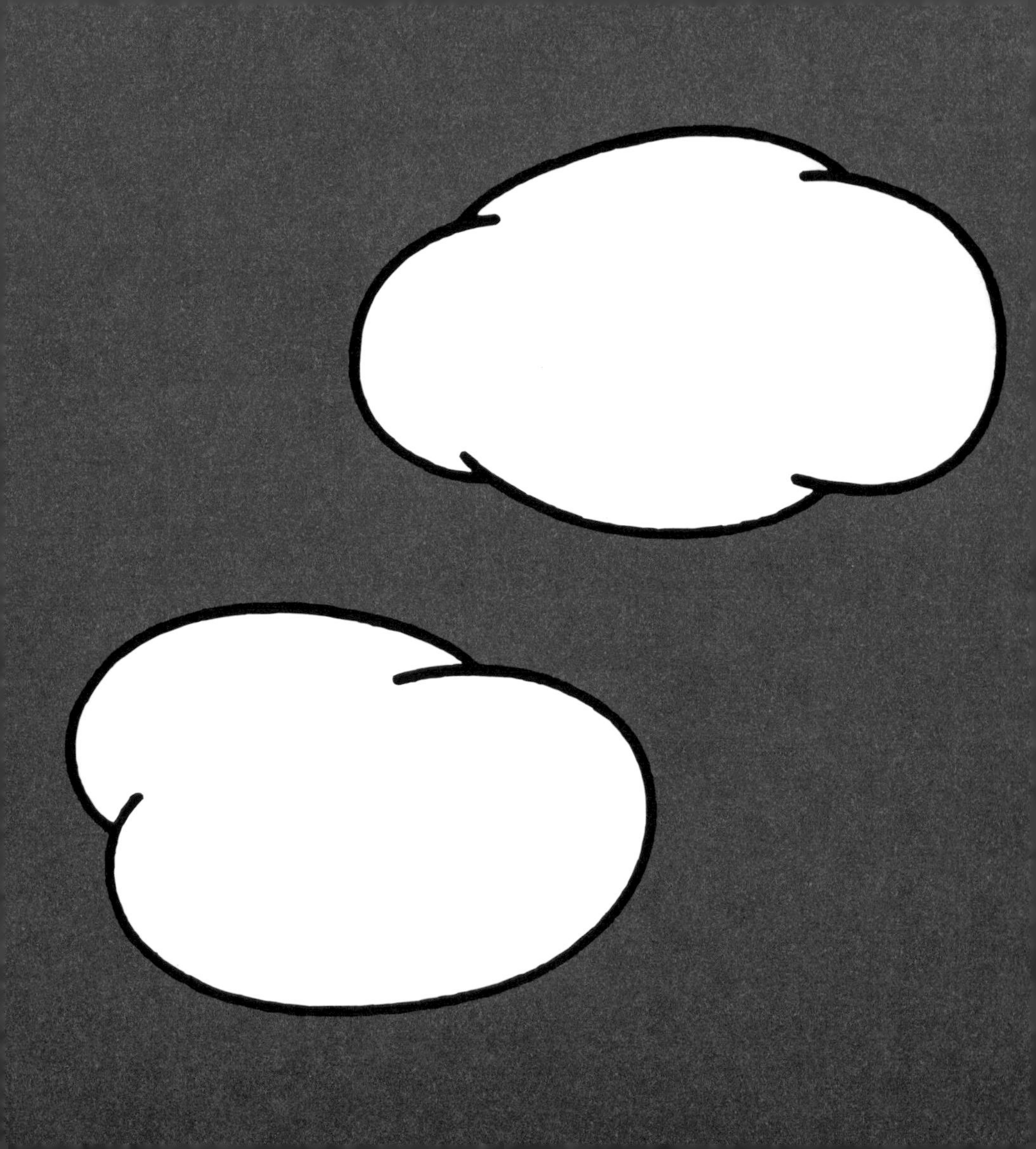

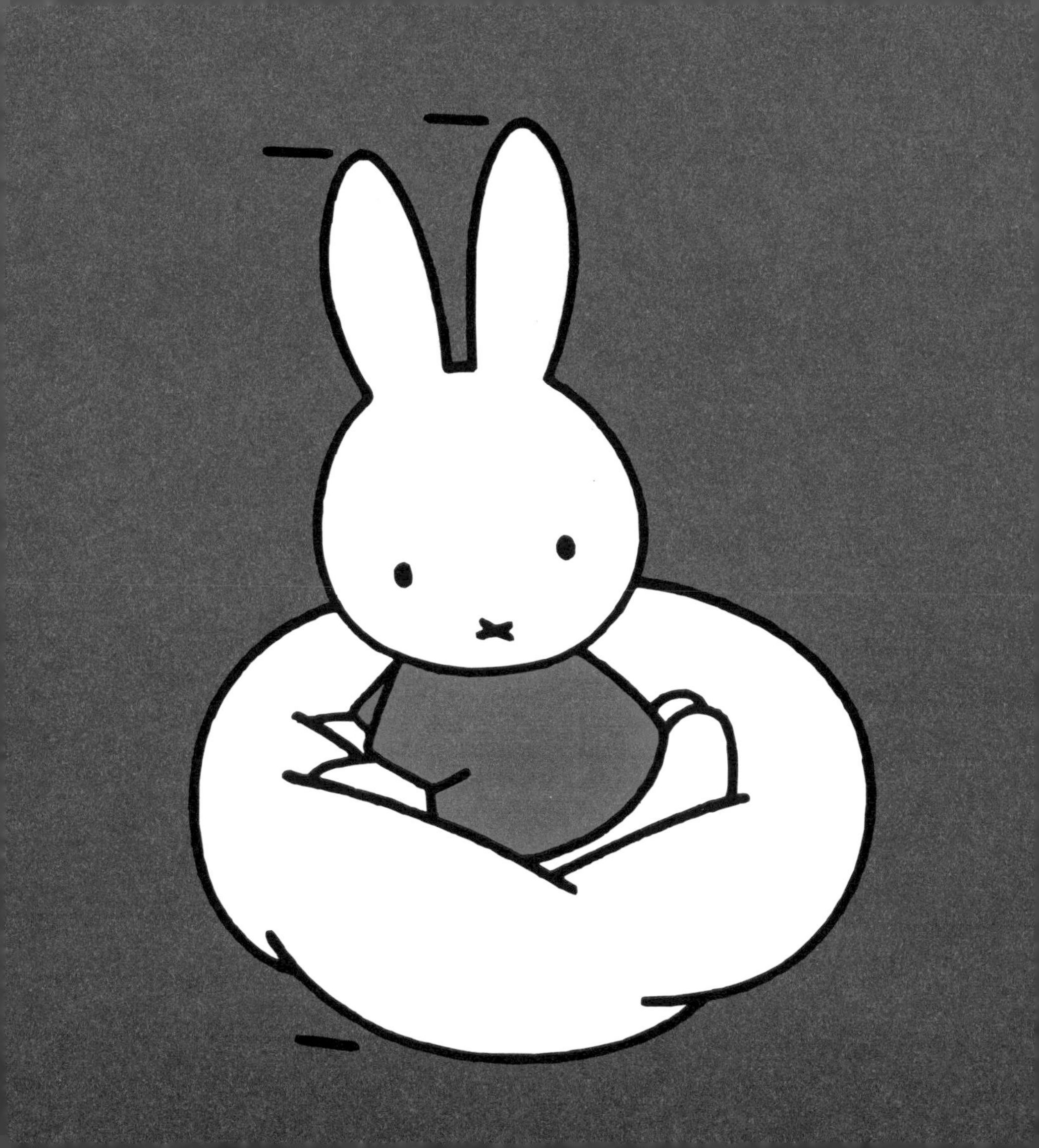

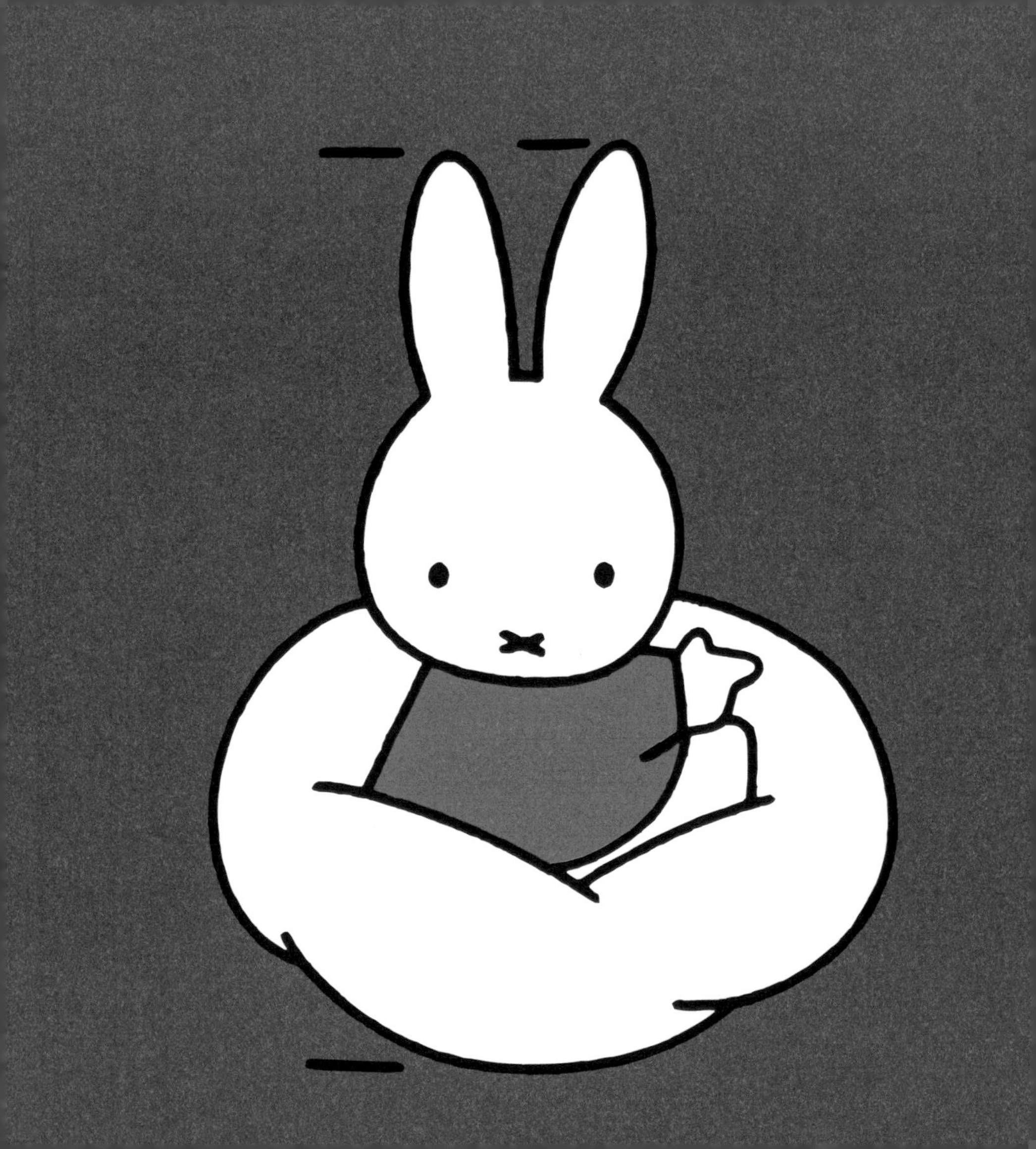

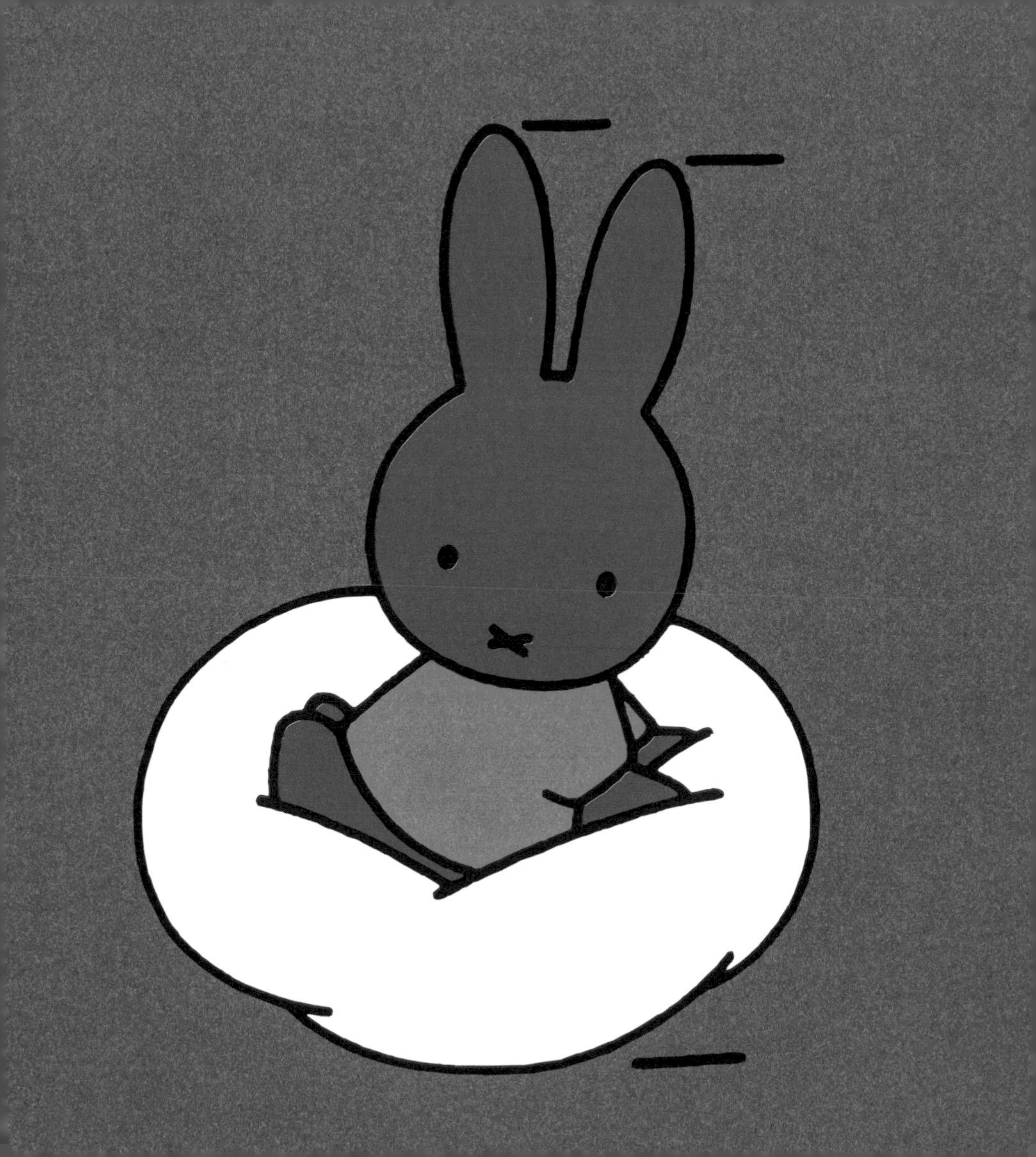

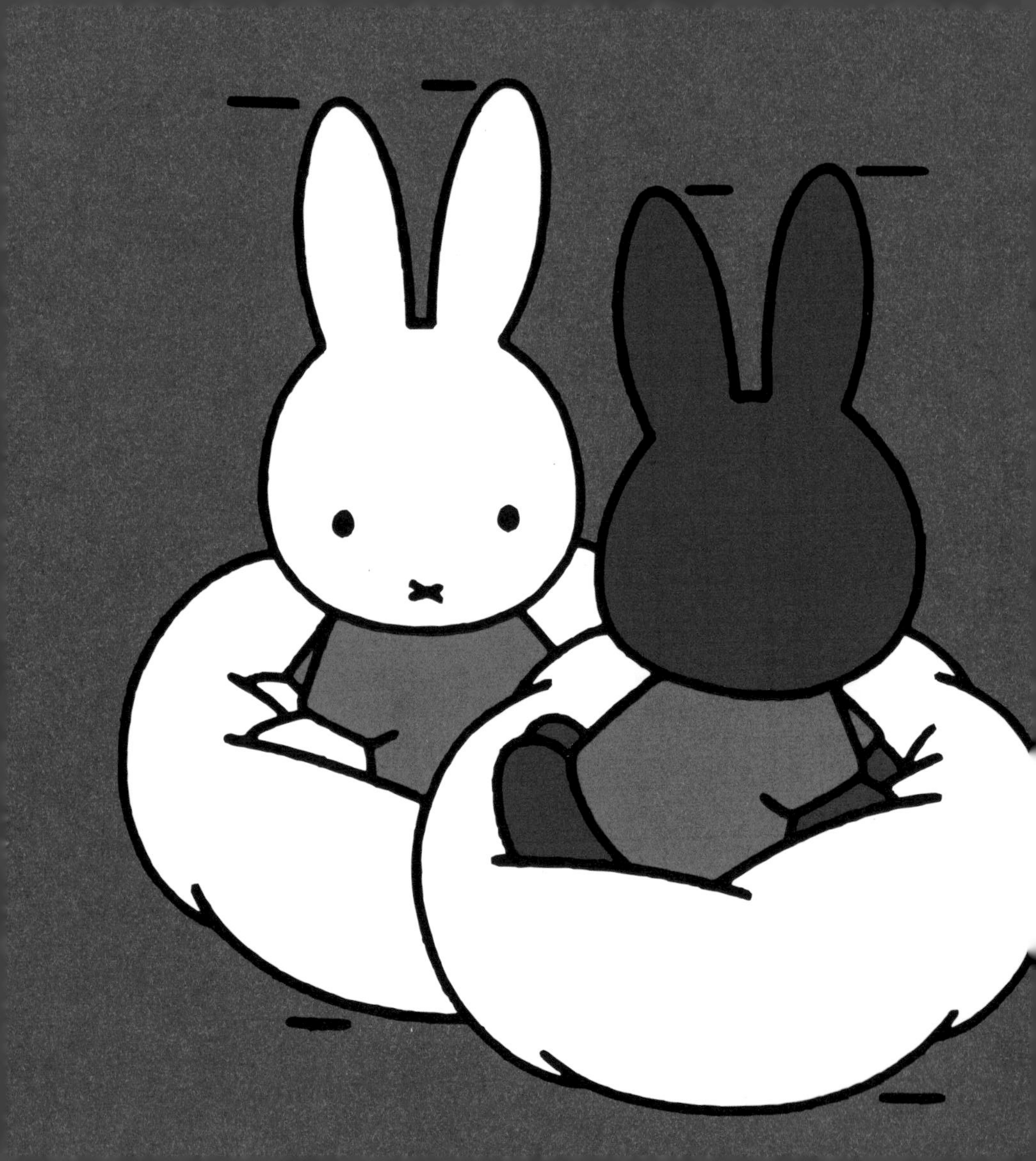

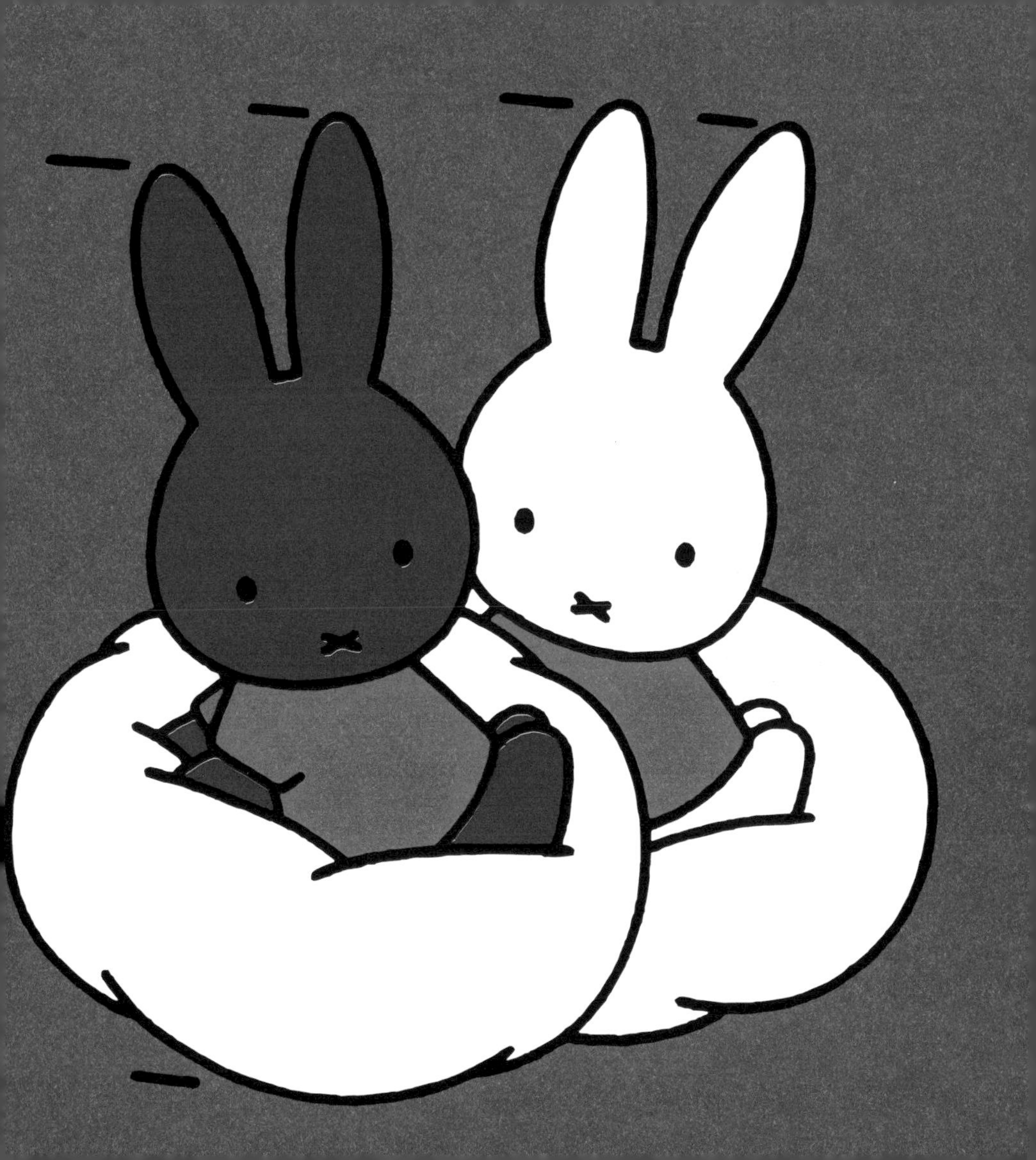

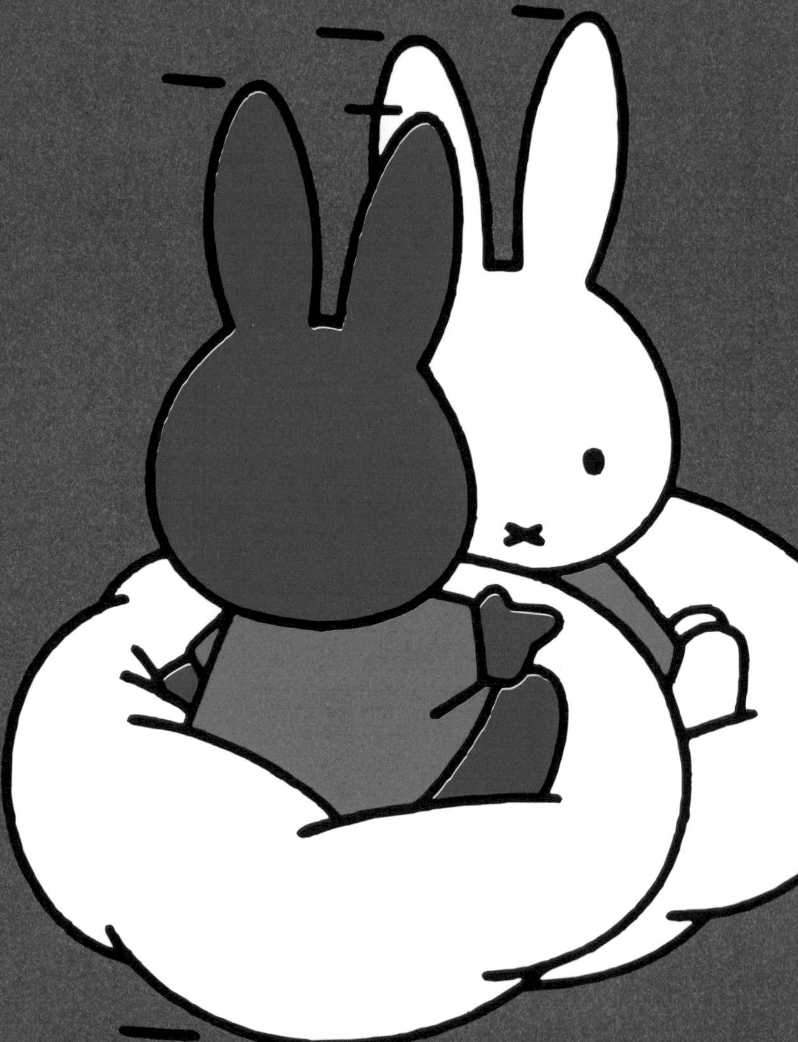

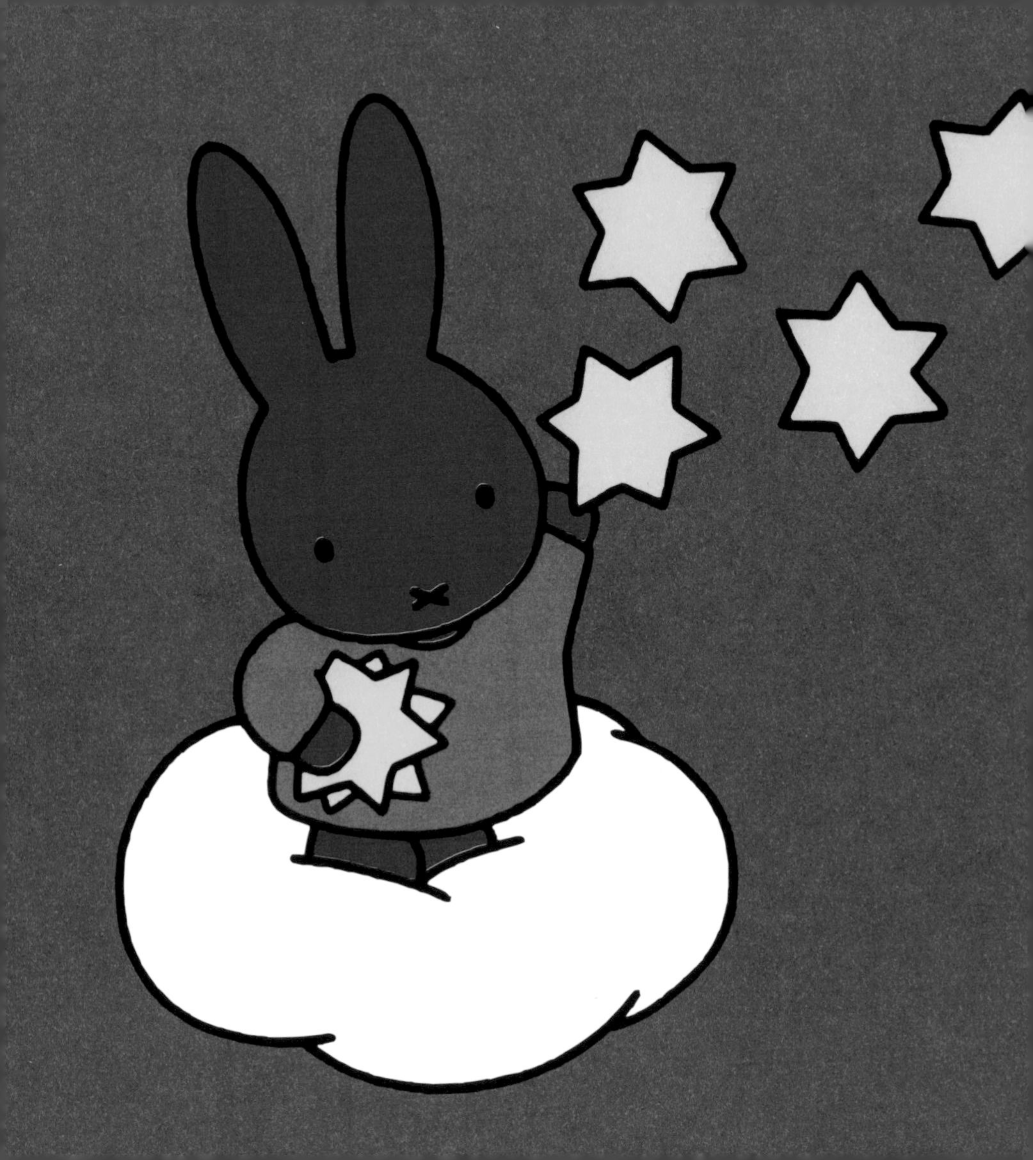

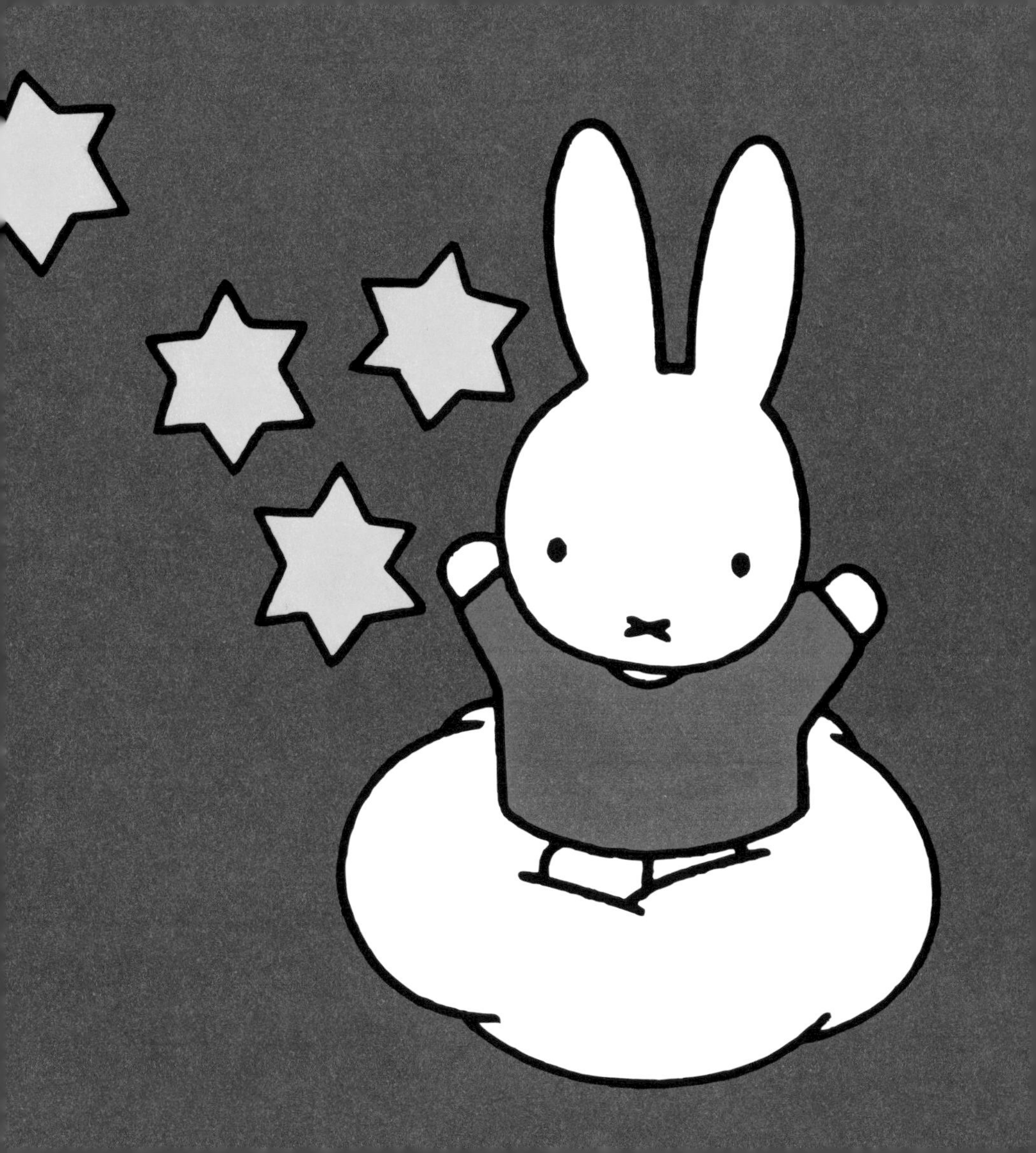

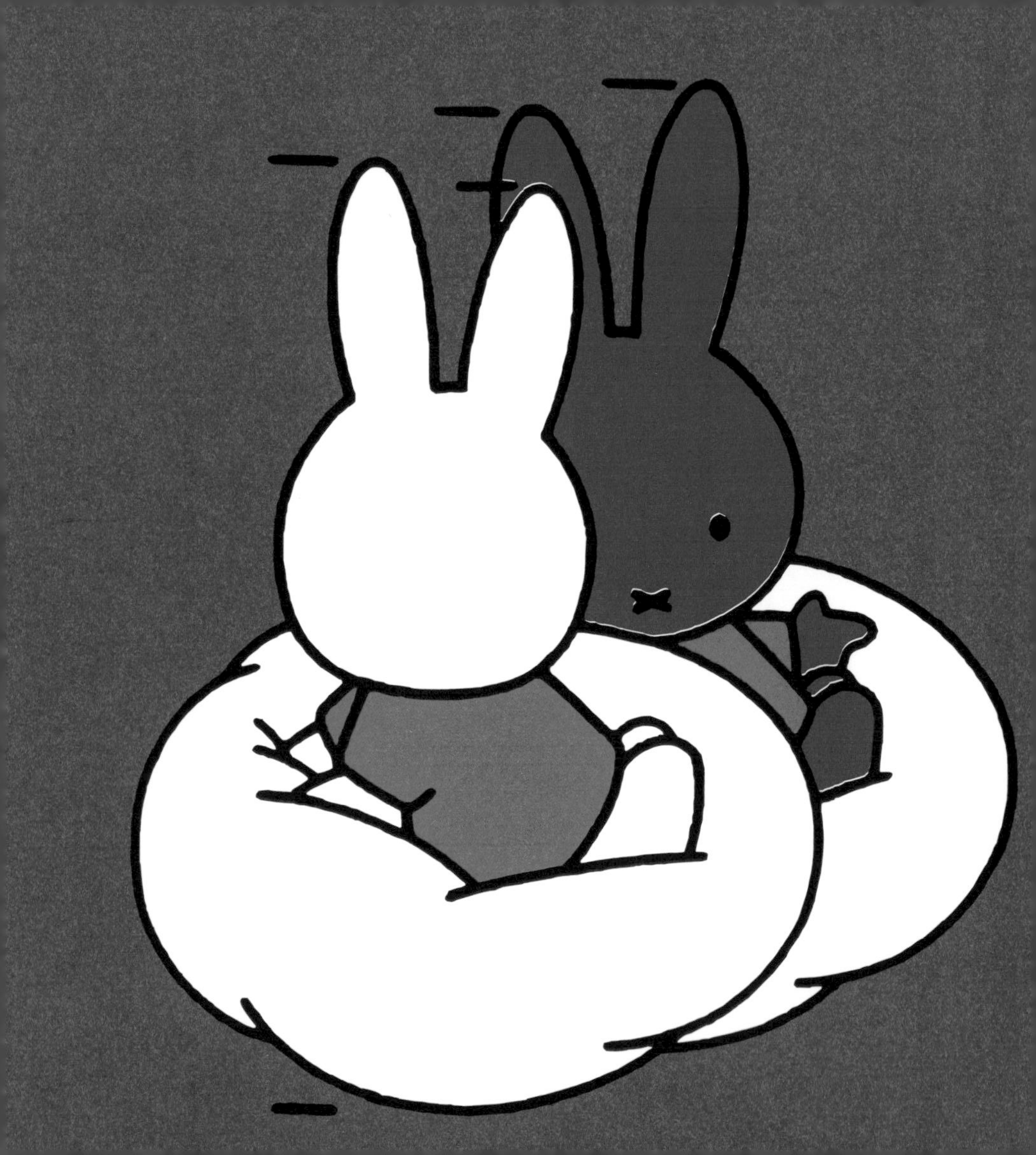

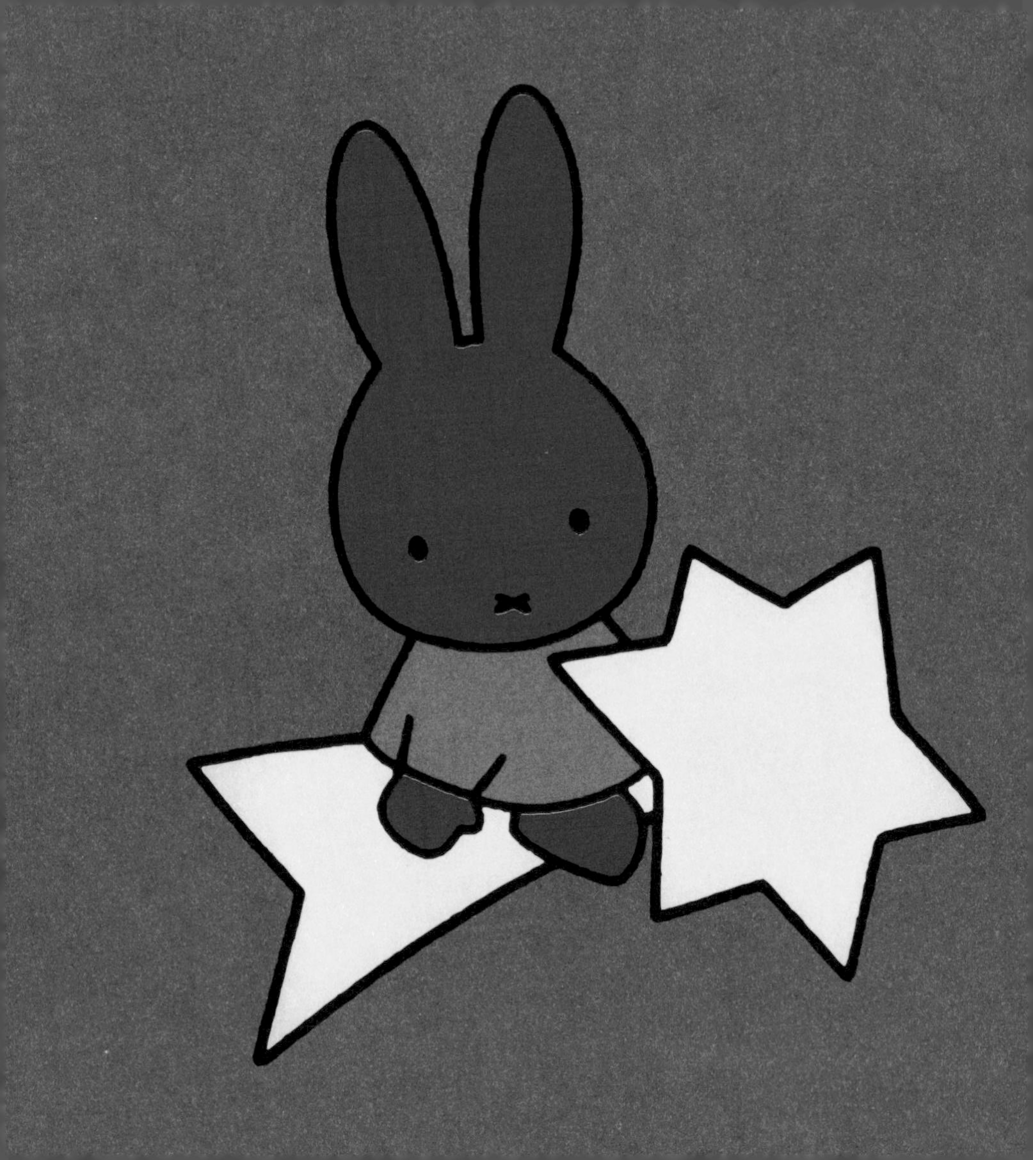

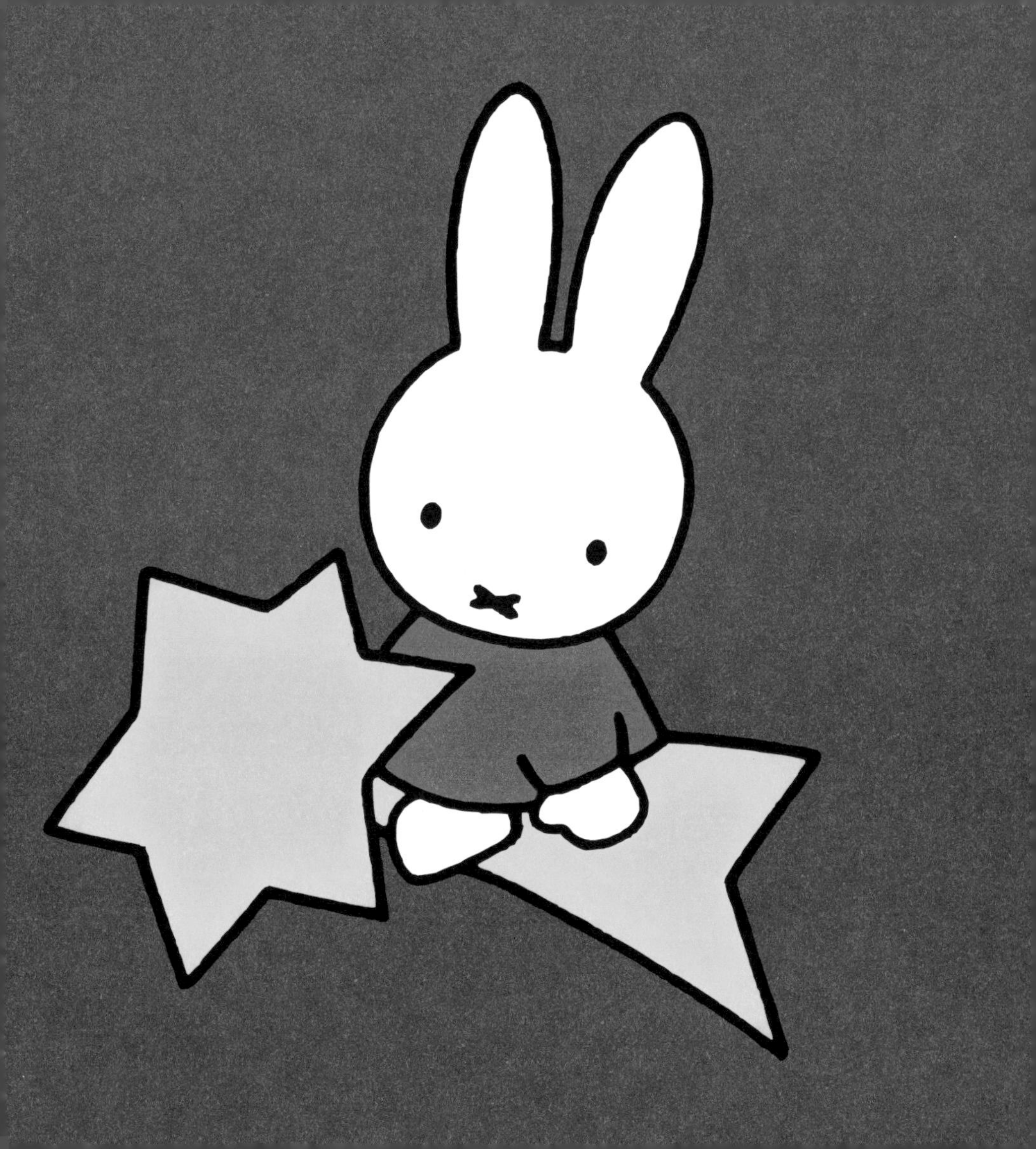

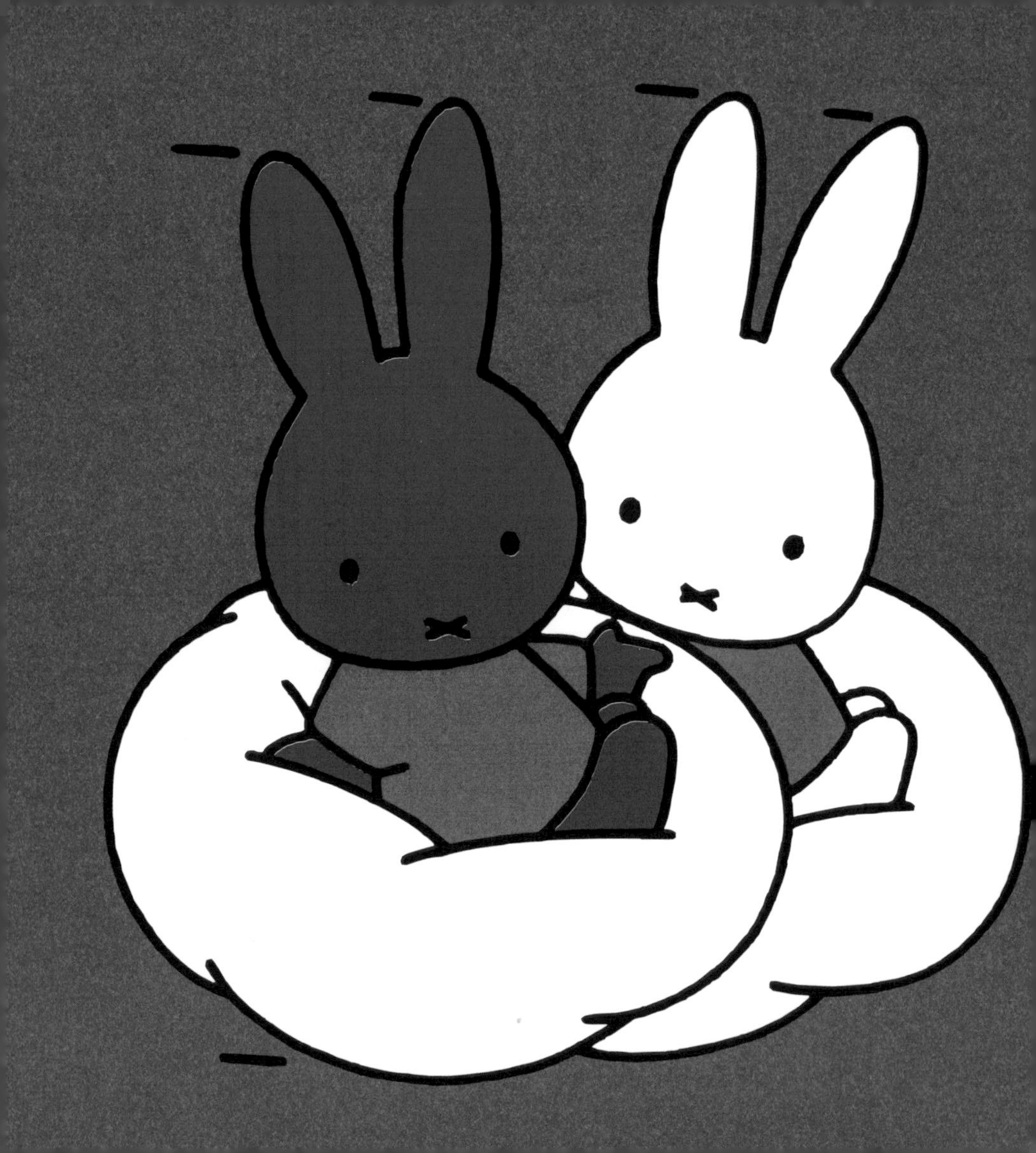

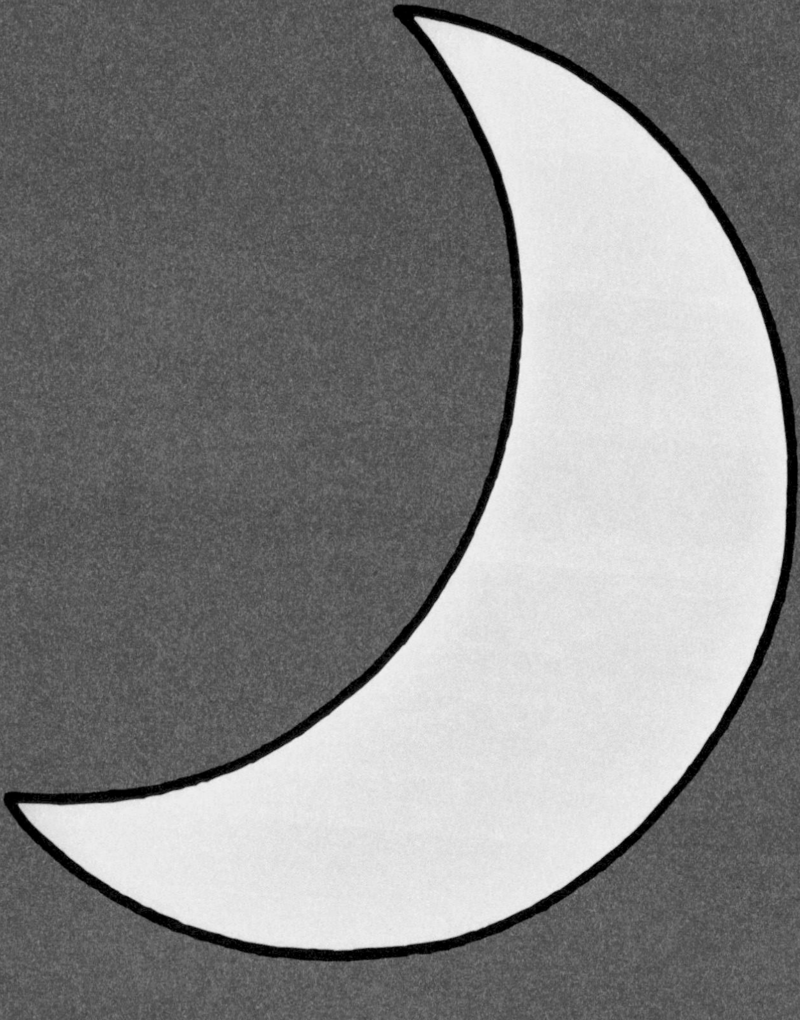

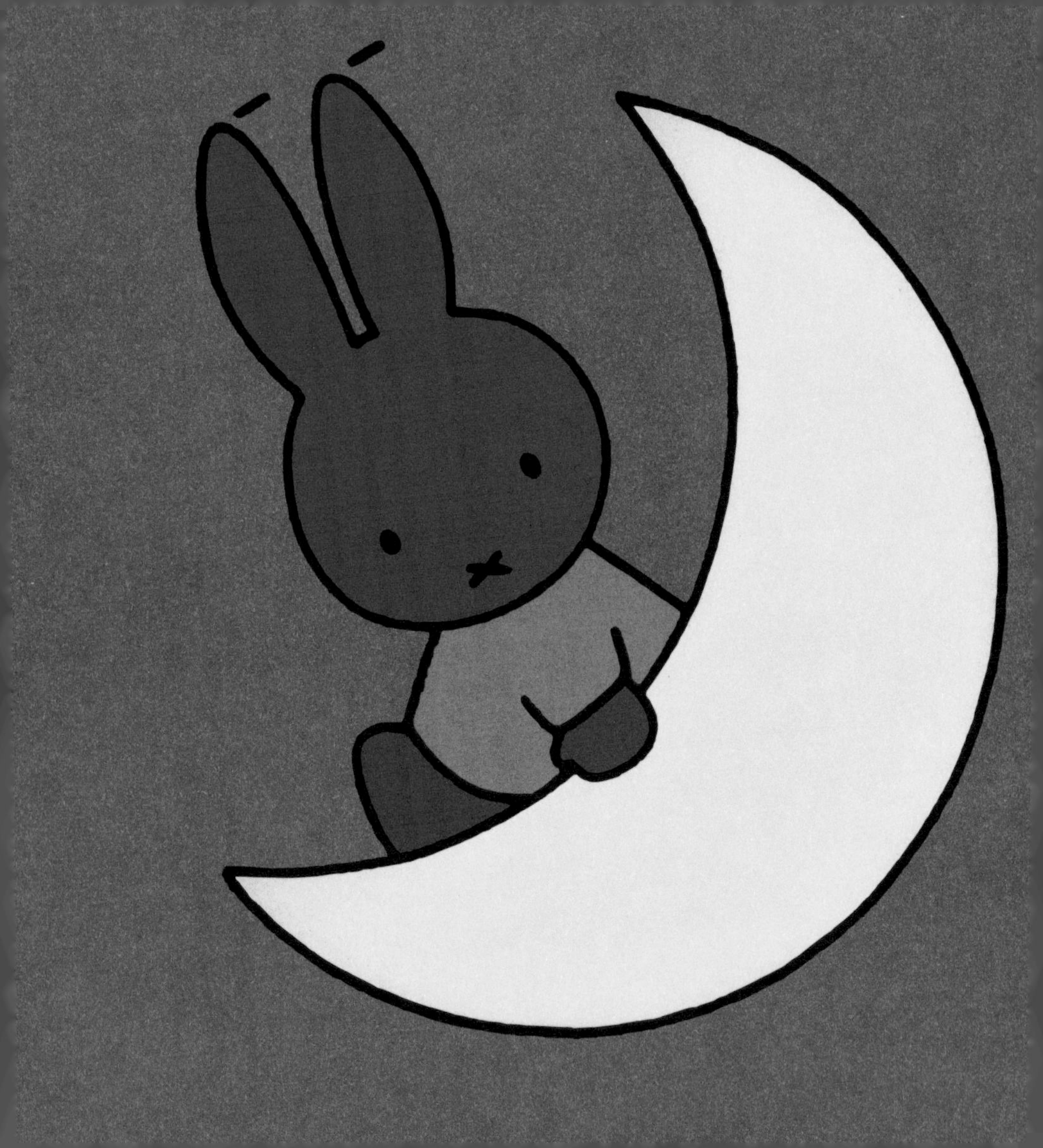

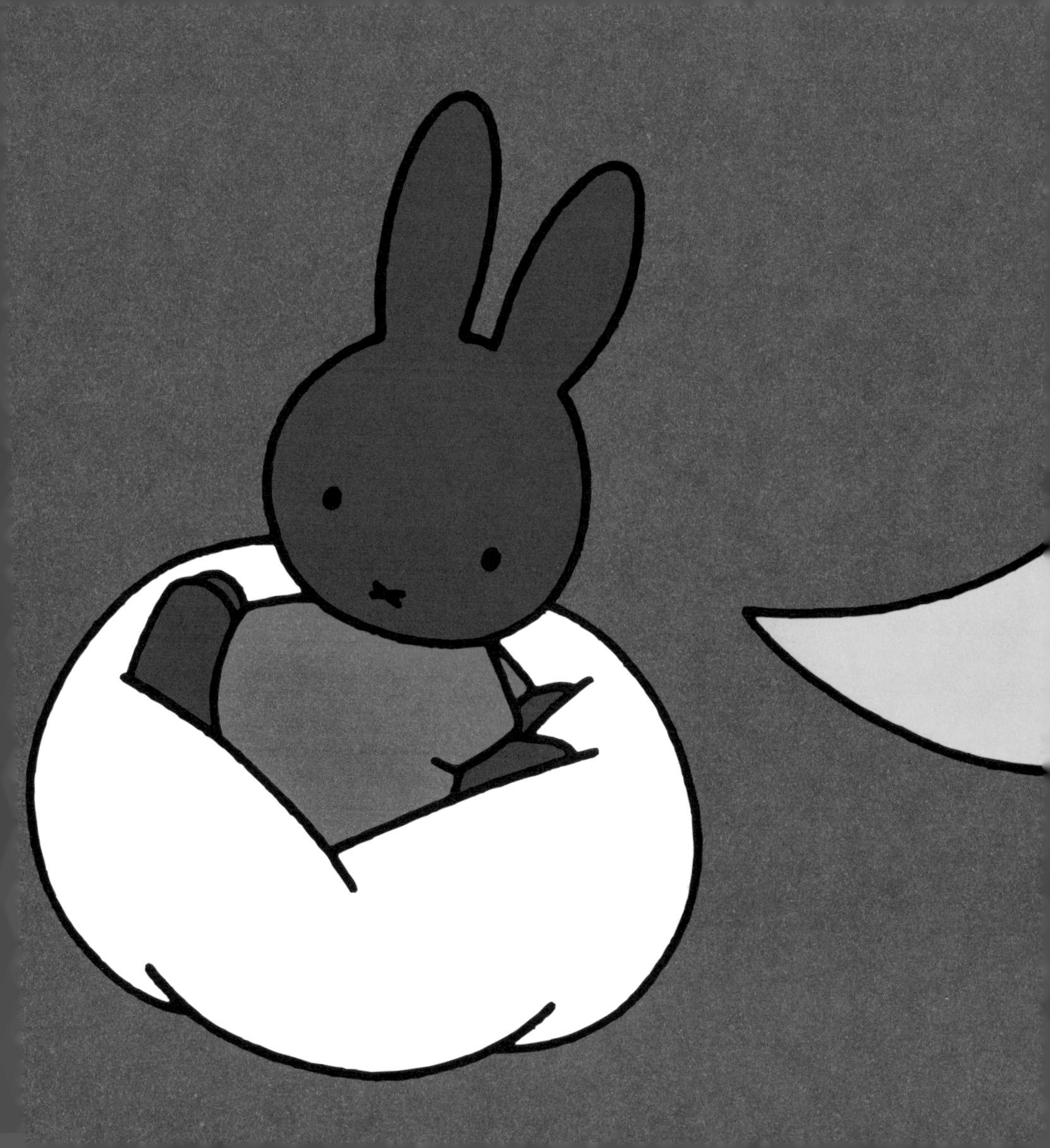

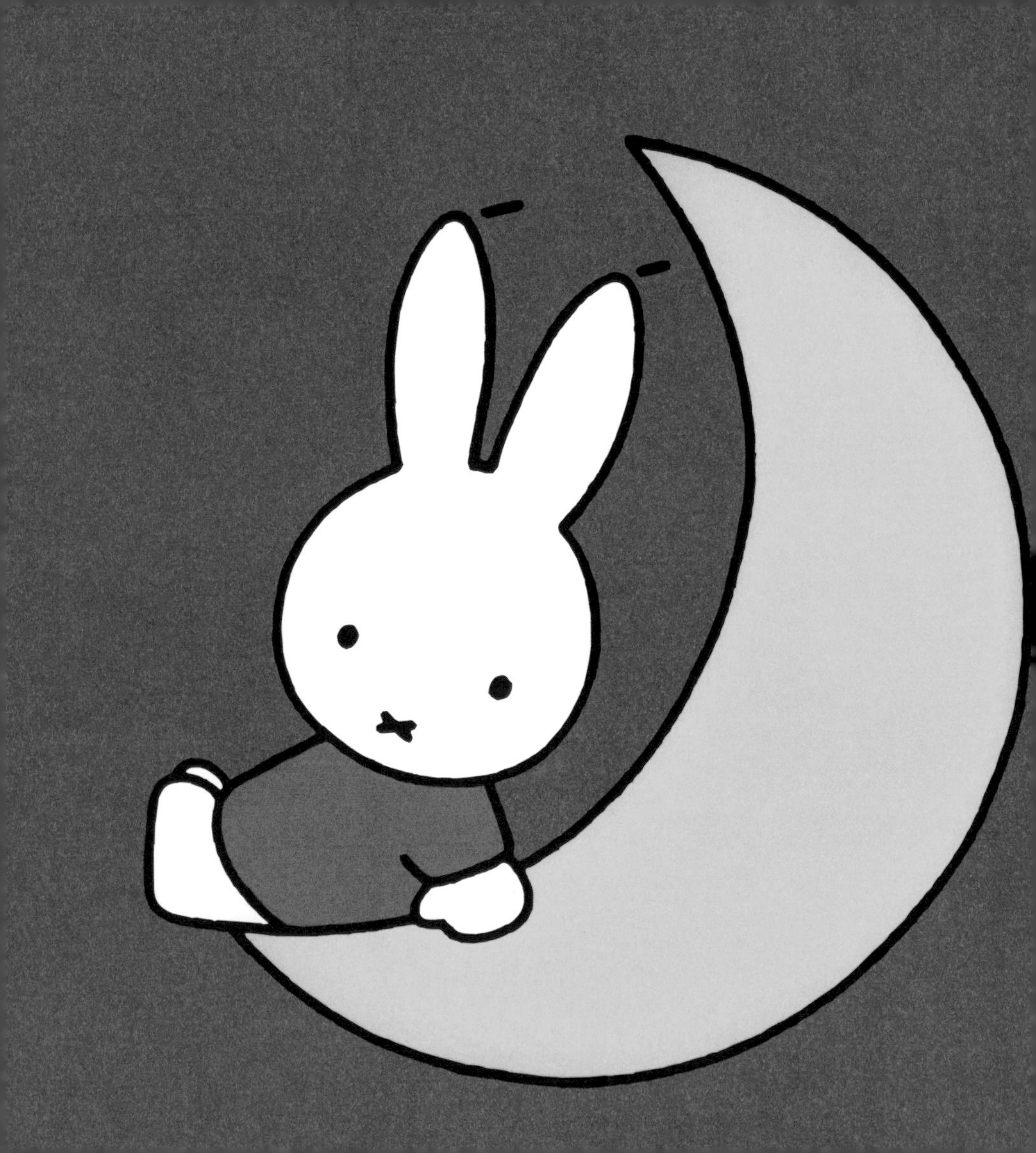

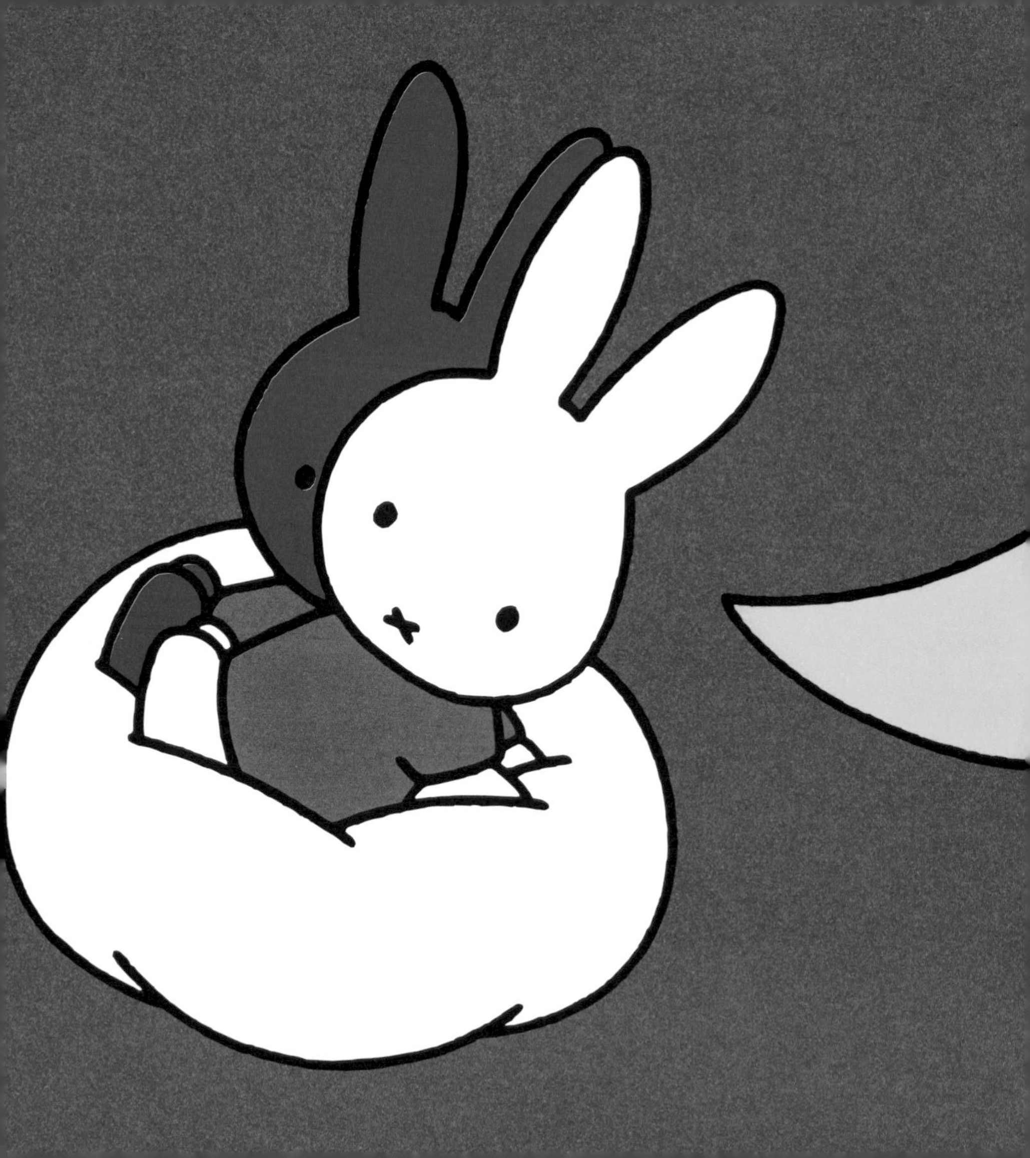

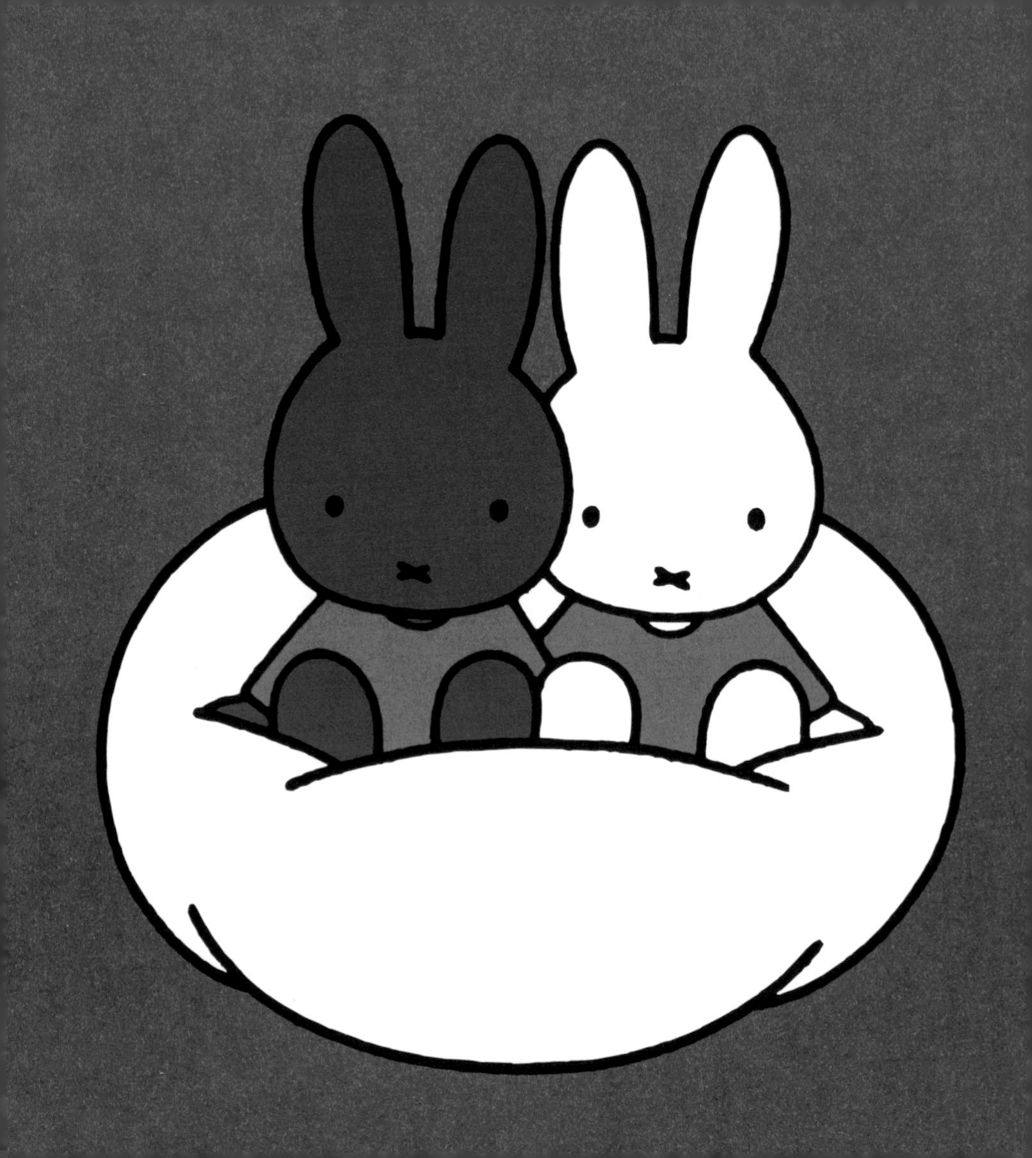

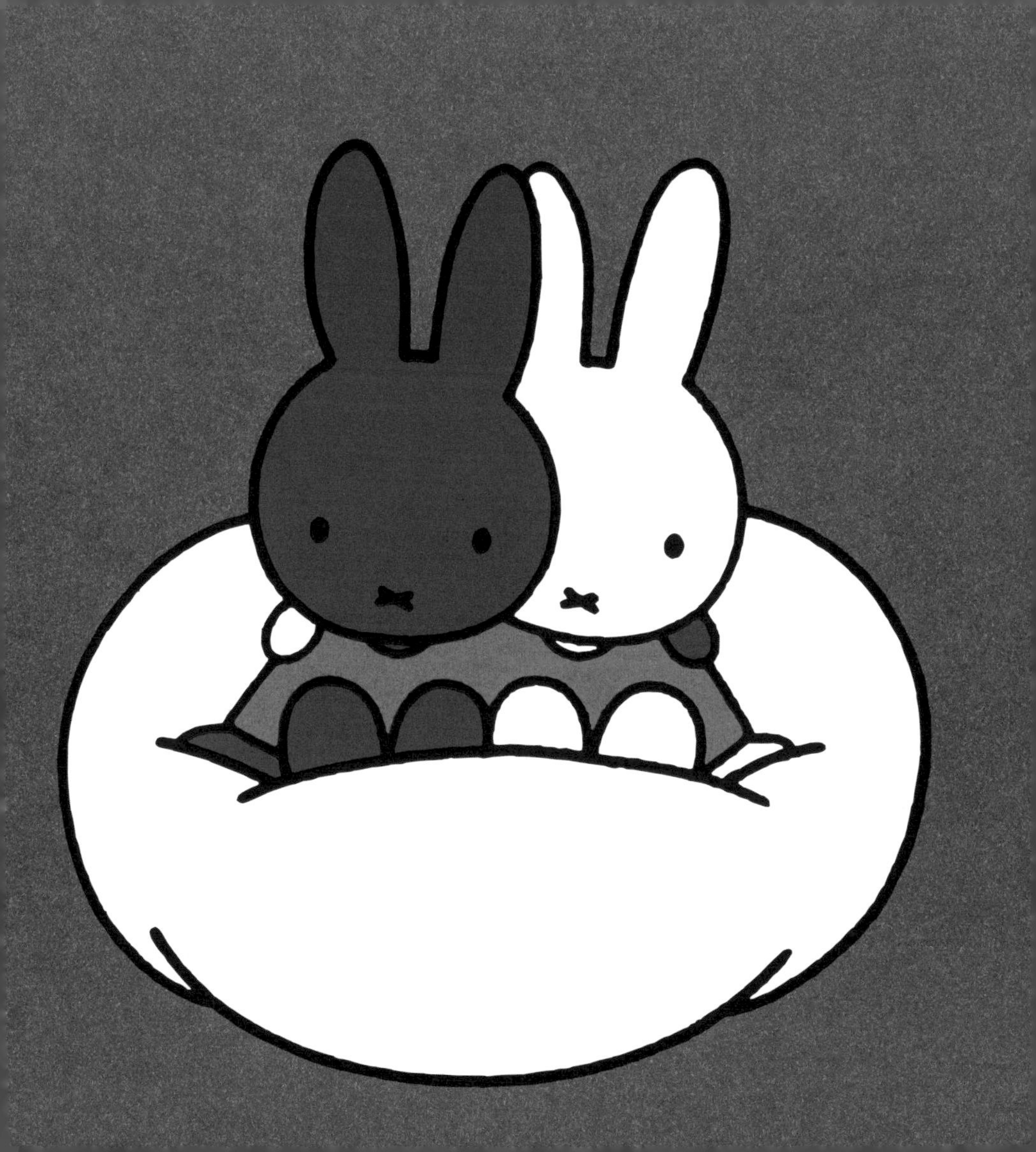

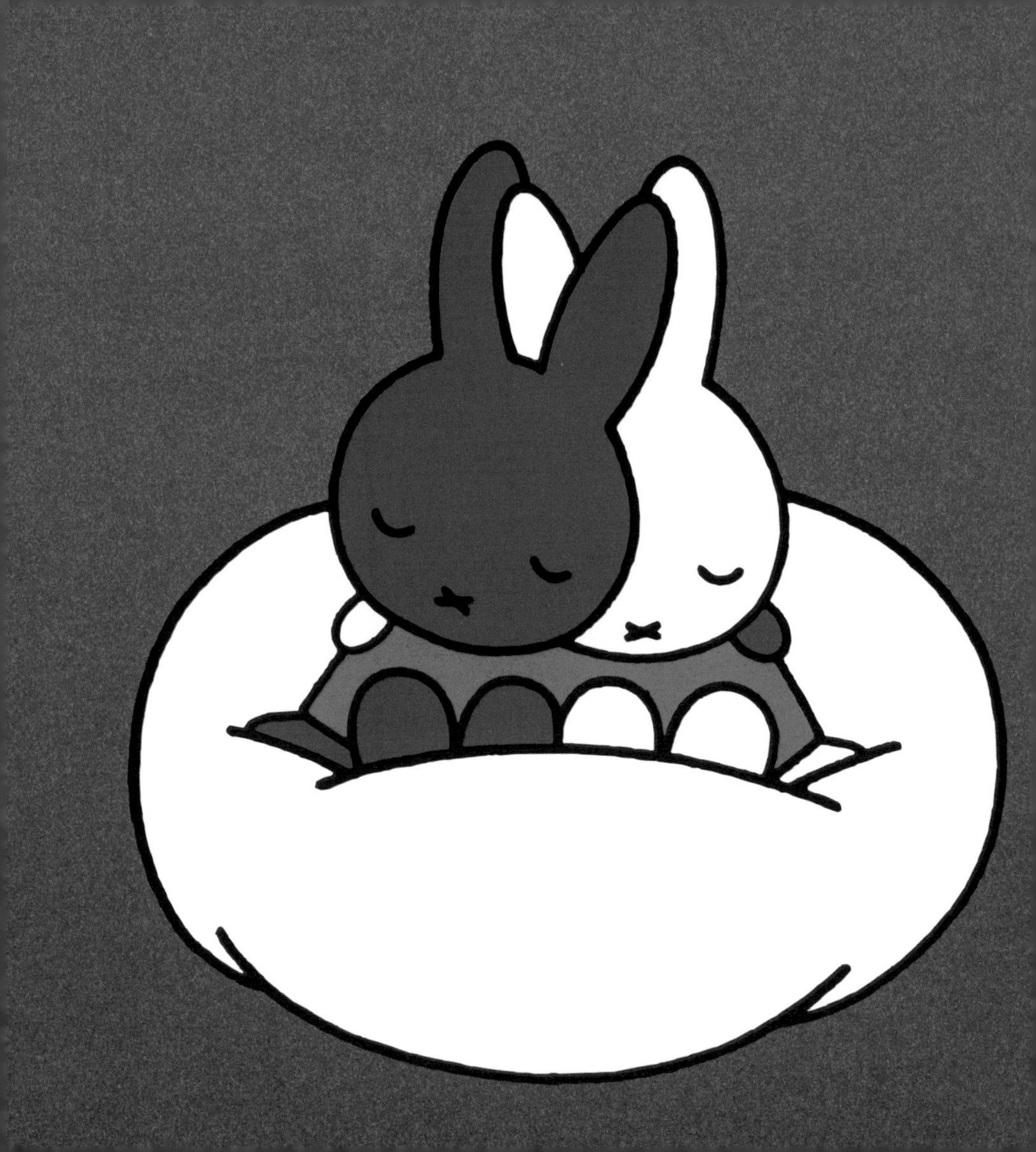